Ladybird  Readers

Alice in Wonderland

Series Editor: Sorrel Pitts
Text adapted by Sorrel Pitts
Illustrated by Barbara Bongini

LADYBIRD BOOKS

UK | USA | Canada | Ireland | Australia
India | New Zealand | South Africa

Ladybird Books is part of the Penguin Random House group of companies
whose addresses can be found at global.penguinrandomhouse.com.
www.penguin.co.uk   www.puffin.co.uk   www.ladybird.co.uk

Penguin
Random House
UK

First published 2017
001

Printed in China

A CIP catalogue record for this book is available from the British Library

ISBN: 978-0-241-28431-5

MIX
Paper from
responsible sources
FSC® C018179

Ladybird Readers

Alice in Wonderland

Picture words

Alice

the White
Rabbit

the Queen
of Hearts

the Knave
of Hearts

the Duchess

the Mad Hatter

rabbit hole   tear   the caterpillar

mushroom   playing cards   croquet

pig   trial   tarts

It was a hot day, and Alice wanted to play with her sister.

"It's too hot," said her sister.

Alice was hot, too. She began to feel very, very tired.

Suddenly, a white rabbit ran past.

"Oh, no!" said the White Rabbit. "I'm late!" Then, he ran into a rabbit hole.

Alice jumped into the hole after him. She fell down, down, down, until she came to the bottom.

"That was very strange," she said to herself.

Alice was in a big room. There were lots of doors around her, but she couldn't open them. There was a table in the middle of the room. It had a small key on it.

Then, Alice saw a much smaller door. The key opened the door, but Alice was too big to go through it.

Alice looked at the table again. Now, there was a bottle on it. The bottle had writing that said DRINK ME. Alice put the key on the table, and drank from the bottle.

"OH!" she said. "I feel very strange!" Suddenly, Alice was getting smaller and smaller!

13

Soon, Alice was so small that she could get through the little door. But the key was still on the table, and now she couldn't get it!

Then, Alice saw a little cake with EAT ME written on it. She ate the cake, and this time she grew bigger and bigger.

Now, Alice could get the key from the table, but she was too big to go through the door. Suddenly, the White Rabbit came into the room.

"Can you help me?" Alice asked.

But when the White Rabbit saw her, he ran away.

"I do feel very strange," Alice said.

Alice was getting smaller and smaller again. She began to cry, and lots of tears fell from her eyes. Soon, she was swimming in tears!

While she was swimming out of the tears, Alice saw some animals.

"That's very strange!" she said to herself.

19

Alice saw a caterpillar on
a mushroom.

"Can you make me big again?" she
asked the caterpillar.

"One side will make you bigger,"
said the caterpillar, "and the other
side will make you smaller."

"One side of what?" asked Alice.

"Eat the mushroom," said the caterpillar, and then he left.

Alice ate a bit of the mushroom. She suddenly grew bigger. Then, she put the mushroom in her pocket.

Next, Alice saw a house.
She went inside it.

In the house was the Duchess
with a baby and a cat.

The cat smiled at Alice.

25

Suddenly, the Duchess jumped up. "Come here!" she said to Alice. "You can have the baby. I'm going to play a game of croquet with the Queen!"

Alice looked at the baby. But it wasn't a baby now, it was a pig. It jumped out of the Duchess's arms, and ran away!

27

Alice found the cat in a tree.

"Are you going to play croquet with the Queen?" he asked Alice.

"I don't know," she said.

"I am," smiled the cat. He left, but his smile stayed. It was very strange!

29

Next, Alice found the Mad Hatter and his friends. They were drinking tea and eating cake.

Alice drank some tea with them.

31

Then, Alice saw a tree with a door in it. When she went through the door, she was back in the room with the table. The key to the little door was still on the table.

"This time I know what to do," said Alice. She took the key. Then, she took the mushroom from her pocket and ate it. She became smaller and smaller, until she could get through the little door.

Alice saw some playing cards. There were some white flowers in the trees, and the playing cards were painting the flowers red.

"Why are you painting the flowers red?" asked Alice.

"The Queen of Hearts wants all flowers to be red," they said.

Soon, the Queen of Hearts came past Alice. She was with the Duchess and the White Rabbit.

The Queen looked at the white flowers and then at the playing cards.

"Cut off their heads," she said. "Then, I want to play a game of croquet!"

39

It was a very strange game of croquet. When it was finished, only the Queen and Alice were still in the garden.

"Now for the trial," said the Queen.

The Knave of Hearts was on trial.

"He took my tarts!" said the Queen. "Cut off his head!"

"You can't do that!" said Alice.

"I can!" said the Queen. "And now I'm going to cut off your head, too!"

"No!" said Alice. "No, no, NO!"

"Wake up! Wake up, Alice!"

Suddenly, Alice was back with her sister.

"OH!" she said, "I've just had a very strange dream . . ."

Activities

The key below describes the skills practiced in each activity.

 Spelling and writing

 Reading

 Speaking

 Critical thinking

 Preparation for the Cambridge Young Learners Exams

1 **Choose the correct words and write them on the lines.**

the caterpillar   tears   playing cards   mushroom

1 When we cry, these come out of our eyes. _____tears_____

2 A long, green insect. _____

3 This plant grows under trees. _____

4 People use these in games they play at a table. _____

2 Look and read. Write *yes* or *no*.

It was a hot day and Alice wanted to play with her sister.

"It's too hot," said her sister.

Alice was hot, too. She began to feel very, very tired.

Suddenly, a white rabbit ran past.

1 It was a hot day, but Alice wanted to play with her sister.

.......yes.......

2 Alice's sister did not want to play, because it was too hot.

....

3 A white rabbit in a blue jacket ran past.

....

4 The white rabbit was looking at a clock.

....

3 Read the text. Choose the correct words and write them next to 1—4.

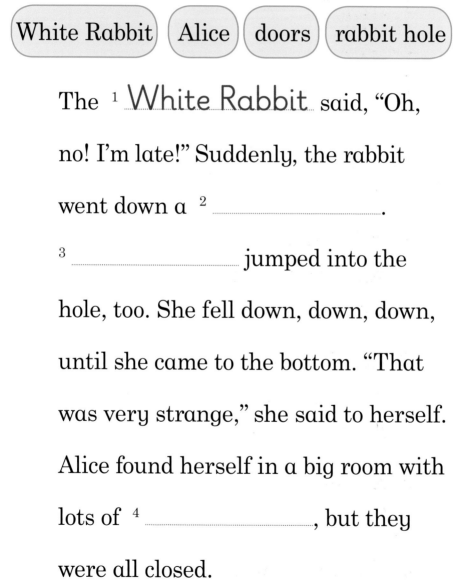

White Rabbit   Alice   doors   rabbit hole

The ¹ <u>White Rabbit</u> said, "Oh, no! I'm late!" Suddenly, the rabbit went down a ² _____.

³ _____ jumped into the hole, too. She fell down, down, down, until she came to the bottom. "That was very strange," she said to herself. Alice found herself in a big room with lots of ⁴ _____, but they were all closed.

4 **Find the words.** 📖

```
p  u  t  w  t  m  a  p  b  s  w  y
l  u  x  f  z  u  f  r  a  x  t  i
a  y  n  d  t  s  i  i  l  e  b  u
y  g  q  b  e  h  n  n  l  k  e  y
i  c  a  t  e  r  p  i  l  l  a  r
n  x  m  h  r  o  i  e  l  p  i  i
g  k  x  x  b  o  g  g  a  s  r  r
c  t  b  e  a  m  t  e  a  r  l  l
a  w  h  i  t  e  r  a  b  b  i  t
r  b (t  a  r  t) m  r  s  w  f  f
d  e  y  e  h  g  s  o  c  a  k  e
s  a  e  u  u  b  q  a  b  m  g  b
```

tart

caterpillar

cake

tear

mushroom

playing
cards

White
Rabbit

pig

5 **Read the answers. Write the questions.**

1 What did Alice see when she looked at the table again?

She saw a bottle.

2 What writing ....

....?

It had writing that said DRINK ME.

3 Who ....

....?

The White Rabbit came into the room.

4 How ....?

She felt very strange.

6 **Read the text. Choose the correct words and write them on the lines.**

1 very	too	so
2 yet	still	ever
3 couldn't	could	can't
4 wrote	written	was written

Soon, Alice was [1] _____so_____ small that she couldn't get through the little door. The key was [2] _____ on the table.

Alice was smaller than the table so she [3] _____ get the key.

Then, Alice saw a little cake with the words EAT ME [4] _____ on it.

1 Now, Alice could get the key from the table, because she had grown bigger and bigger. ....T....

2 But then, she was too big to go through the little door. ....

3 When the White Rabbit came into the room, Alice asked him for the key. ....

4 When the White Rabbit saw Alice in the room, he jumped down the rabbit hole. ....

8 **Ask and answer the questions with a friend.**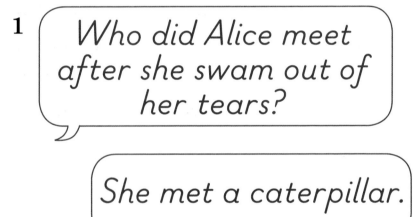

1 *Who did Alice meet after she swam out of her tears?*

She met a caterpillar.

2 Where was the caterpillar?

3 What did Alice say to the caterpillar?

4 What was the caterpillar's answer?

5 How did Alice feel, do you think?

9 Read the text. Write some words to complete the sentences about the story. 📖 ✏️ ✴️

> After Alice ate the mushroom, she suddenly grew bigger.
> Next, she saw a house and went inside it. There, she saw the Duchess with lots of hair on the top of her head and with a baby in her arms. The cat was on the table next to the Duchess. He smiled at Alice.

1 The mushroom made Alice grow _____bigger_____.

2 Alice went into a house where she saw _____.

3 The cat _____.

10 Look at the picture. Put a ✓ or a ✗ in the boxes. 📖 ❓

1 Alice is at the trial. ✓

2 The Queen is very happy. ☐

3 There are three tarts on the table in front of her. ☐

4 The Mad Hatter is on trial. ☐

5 There aren't any animals in the picture. ☐

11 Work with a friend. Talk about the two pictures. How are they different?

a

Next, Alice saw a house. She went inside it.

In the house was a duchess with a baby and a cat.

The cat smiled at Alice.

24

b

Suddenly, the Duchess jumped up. "Come here!" she said to Alice. "You can have the baby. I'm going to play a game of croquet with the Queen!"

Alice looked at the baby. But it wasn't a baby now, it was a pig. It jumped out of the Duchess's arms and ran away!

27

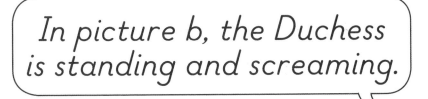

In picture a, the Duchess is sitting in a chair holding a baby.

In picture b, the Duchess is standing and screaming.

12 **Circle the verbs in the past tense.**

Next, Alice found the Mad Hatter and his friends. They were drinking tea and eating cake.

Alice drank some tea with them.

1 Alice **drank** / **drinks** some tea with the Queen.

2 Alice **went** / **goes** through a door in a tree.

3 Alice **takes** / **took** the key and ate some of the mushroom.

4 She **becomes** / **became** smaller and could get through the little door.

5 The playing cards **were** / **are** painting the flowers.

13 Look at the letters. Write the words. 📖 ✏️

i s m g w i n m

1 While Alice was ___swimming___ in tears, she saw some animals.

m r u o s o m h

2 "Eat the _____," said the caterpillar.

d a M H t a t r e

3 The _____ was drinking tea and eating cake.

i n t p n g a i

4 The playing cards were _____ the flowers red.

14 Write *can, can't, could,* or *couldn't.*

1 " Can you make me big again?"
Alice asked the caterpillar.

2 Alice .... see lots of doors
around her.

3 But they were closed and she
.... open them.

4 "You .... do that!" said
Alice to the Queen of Hearts.

5 "I ....!" said the Queen,
"And now I'm going to cut off your
head, too!"

15 Choose the best answers. 📖 ✿

1 "He took my tarts! Cut off his head," said

(**a** the Queen.)   **b** the Knave of Hearts.

2 "You can't do that!" said

a Alice.   **b** the playing cards.

3 "Wake up! Wake up, Alice!" said

a the Queen.   **b** Alice's sister.

4 "OH! I've just had a very strange dream," said

a Alice.   **b** Alice's sister.

16 **Read the text and choose the best answers. Write a—d.**

a "OH! I've just had a very strange dream."

b "I don't know."

c "The Queen only likes red ones."

d "It's too hot."

1 Alice: "Let's play a game!"
Alice's sister: _____d_____

2 The cat: "Are you going to play croquet with the Queen?"
Alice: _____

3 Alice: "Why are you painting the flowers red?"
Playing card: _____

4 Alice's sister: "Wake up! Wake up, Alice!"
Alice: _____

17 **Read the questions. Write complete answers.** 📖 ✏️ ❓

1 Why was the Knave of Hearts on trial?

He was on trial because he took the Queen's tarts.

2 What do we learn at the end of the story?

_____

_____

3 Why did so many strange things happen to Alice in Wonderland, do you think?

_____

_____

Level 4

The Pied Piper of Hamelin

978–0–241–25378–6 ☐

The Wizard of Oz

978–0–241–25379–3 ☐

Sam and the Robots

978–0–241–25380-9 ☐

Space

978–0–241–25381–6 ☐

Pinocchio

978–0–241–28430–8 ☐

Alice in Wonderland

978–0–241–28431–5 ☐

Knights and Castles

978–0–241–28432–2 ☐

Heidi

978–0–241–28433–9 ☐

Peter and the Wolf

978–0–241–28434–6 ☐